Amelia the Potted Flower

By: Billen Barre

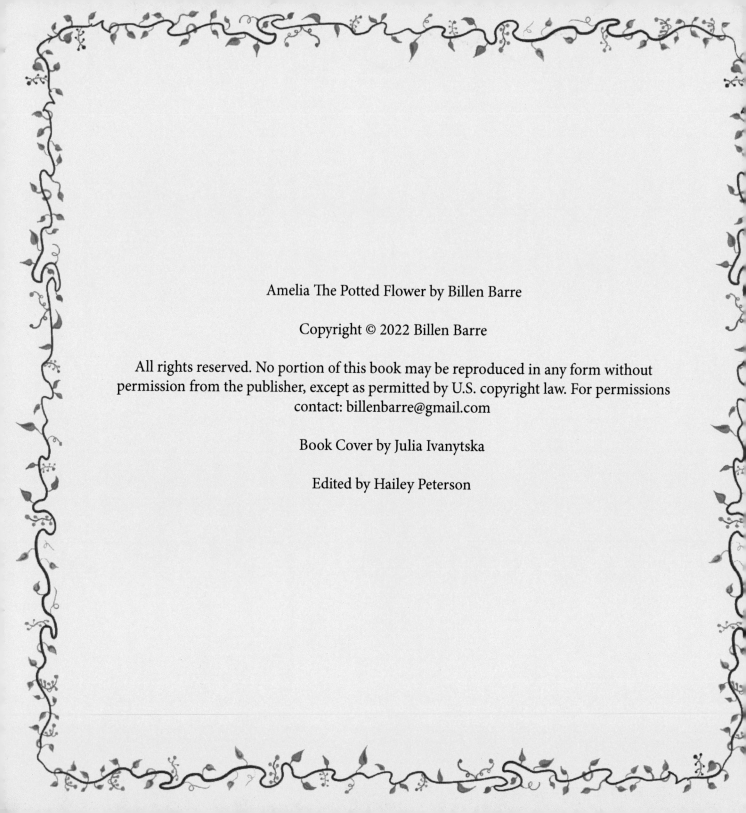

Amelia The Potted Flower by Billen Barre

Copyright © 2022 Billen Barre

Book Cover by Julia Ivanytska

Edited by Hailey Peterson

About the Book

Join Amelia on her road to self-discovery and see the friends she makes along the way! Amelia teaches every child patience, the importance of friendship, and the value of self-discovery.

"GOOD MORNING!!"

Shouted Amelia from her yellow pot on the porch.

"It's a beautiful morning!" said Rosie the Rose.

Ollie the Cat came prancing outside and sat next to Amelia.

"How was your night, Amelia?" asked Ollie.

"What are you asking her for?" Sunny the Sunflower said rudely. "Amelia didn't feel the rain last night since she sits in her fancy pot under the porch roof."

Amelia ignored her but was hurt.

"I had a great night! I couldn't feel the rain, but it was nice to watch," she said.

"Amelia, look! I'm starting to bloom!" Daphne the Daffodil shouted.

"Oh, you look beautiful, Daphne!" said Amelia.

Amelia smiled but was sad on the inside. She was planted four years ago but she hadn't bloomed yet.

Everyone in the garden had tried to find out what kind of flower Amelia was.

Ollie had even brought a book about flowers so they could see if she was in it, but none of the pictures looked like her.

Ollie could tell Amelia was sad.

"You will bloom when it's the right time for you," Ollie said.

Suddenly, Bumble the Bumblebee bumped into Amelia's pot.

"Do you know who you should talk to? Miss Oakwood! She might know what kind of flower you are!" said Bumble.

"Miss Oakwood is older than anybody I know, besides Mr. Tortle the Tortoise, but he's away on holiday."

"How is she supposed to get to Miss Oakwood?" Sunny retorted.

"I have an idea!" Ollie shouted. "We'll take you in this wagon! I can push you there!"

"WOOHOO!!" cheered Amelia. "Let's do this!"

Amelia yelled happily as she zoomed down the porch and slowed to a stop in front of the tomato garden.

"Why hello, what are you all doing over here?" asked Mrs. Sprout brightly.

"Hello, Mrs. Sprout, we are on our way to see Miss Oakwood," Ollie said.

"Oh, that sounds nice! Don't stay out too late; there's a storm coming. I can feel it in my vines," Mrs. Sprout said seriously.

They looked at the clear blue sky above but didn't say anything. "We'll make sure to come back soon!"

They left the garden through a hole in the fence and were on their way.

"Just wait till you see the stream. It's so beautiful!" said Bumble.

Ollie and Bumble knew many different animals outside of the garden.

They introduced Amelia to a bunny, a squirrel, and a couple of birds.

Amelia started to feel nervous. What if Miss Oakwood didn't know what kind of flower she was? What if she would never bloom?

Amelia didn't like that she didn't know what kind of flower she was. She didn't like that she might never meet another flower like herself.

"Hi, Miss Oakwood!" Ollie called out.

"Hello, Ollie!" said Miss Oakwood. "Who is your friend?"

"Hi, my name is Amelia. I live in the garden and I've never met another flower like me before. I was hoping you would know what kind of flower I am."

"Oh, well let me get a good look at you," Miss Oakwood said.

"I can tell you'll have a lot of petals, a lot more petals than a rose, lily, or tulip. You're clearly not a daisy or a sunflower. Hmmm."

A few other creatures joined in to guess but none of them knew what kind of flower Amelia was.

Amelia was starting to lose hope fast.

"I'm sorry, Sweetie, but I don't know what kind of flower you are," said Miss Oakwood sadly.

The wagon suddenly jolted backward and rolled into the stream.

"AMELIA!" screamed Ollie. She chased after Amelia but she couldn't keep up in the rain.

Amelia floated down the rushing stream.

She crashed into a large rock and rolled out of the stream onto the bank.

A tortoise pulled her to safety.

"What are you doing out in this storm?" said the tortoise.

"I got caught in the stream."

"Oh, I'll stay with you until the storm passes. My name is Mr. Tortle," said the tortoise.

This was the tortoise Bumble was talking about!

"Mr. Tortle, I'm sure you've travelled a lot! Have you seen any flowers that look like me? I'm the only flower in my garden that hasn't bloomed yet."

"It seems the storm has hit you a little hard, I can see you have at least one pink petal."

"It's a good thing I've gotten to know and see my fair share of flowers. I would know a camellia anywhere!" said Mr. Tortle.

"Camellia? No, my name is Amelia," said Amelia, confused.

"No, you're a camellia flower. Some camellias bloom early, but some bloom even six or seven years after they're planted."

"Thank you so much, Mr. Tortle! This means so much to me!"

"My pleasure, Dear! I know there are some camellias a few days' journey away. They're not in a pot, of course, but I'm sure they would love to meet you."

"Maybe one day I'll be able to visit them!"

"Amelia!!"

A wet Ollie ran around the corner. Amelia was very happy to see her friend and quickly introduced Ollie and Mr. Tortle before they headed for home.

On their way, Amelia told Ollie all about what Mr. Tortle said.

They quickly reached the garden and all the plants oohed and aahed when they saw Amelia's pink petal.

Amelia happily told her friends all about her adventures and proudly showed off her one pink petal.

Now that she knew what kind of flower she was, she didn't feel in a rush to bloom anymore.

Amelia wanted to see more camellias like her one day.

Hopefully Ollie wouldn't mind another trip outside the fence to see them. But they would have to ask Mrs. Sprout about the weather first, just to make sure.